I Like to Read® books, created by award-winning picture book artists as well as talented newcomers, instill confidence and the joy of reading in new readers.

We want to hear every new reader say, "I like to read!"

Visit our website for flash cards, activities, and more about the series:
www.holidayhouse.com/ILiketoRead
#ILTR

This book has been officially leveled by using the F&P Text Level Gradient™ Leveling System.

I LIKE TO READ is a registered trademark of Holiday House Publishing, Inc.

Copyright © 2020 by Susan Batori
All Rights Reserved
HOLIDAY HOUSE is registered in the U.S. Patent and Trademark Office.
Printed and bound in December 2019 at Tien Wah Press, Johor Bahru, Johor, Malaysia.
The artwork was created with digital tools.

www.holidayhouse.com
First Edition
1 3 5 7 9 10 8 6 4 2

This book has been officially leveled by using the F&P Text Level Gradient™ Leveling System.

Library of Congress Cataloging-in-Publication Data
Names: Batori, Susan, author.
Title: It is a tree / Susan Batori.
Other titles: Blind men and the elephant. English.
Description: First edition. | New York : Holiday House, [2020] | Series:
I like to read | Summary: In this retelling of the fable from India,
blindfolded children at a party play a guessing game.
Identifiers: LCCN 2019014107 | ISBN 9780823445318 (hardcover)
Subjects: | CYAC: Fables. | Folklore—India. | Elephants—Folklore.
Classification: LCC PZ8.2.B286 It 2020 | DDC 398.2 [E]—dc23
LC record available at https://lccn.loc.gov/2019014107

It Is a Tree

Susan Batori

I Like to Read®

HOLIDAY HOUSE • NEW YORK

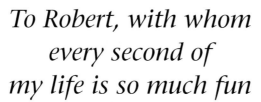

To Robert, with whom
every second of
my life is so much fun

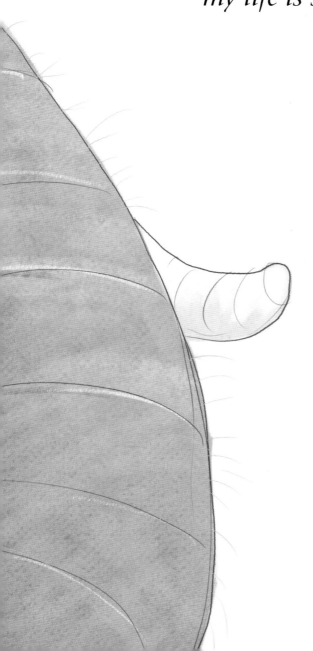

It is a wall.

It is a fan.

A rope.

A tree.

A wall.

A fan.

A pipe.

A snake.

It is an elephant.

I Like to Read®

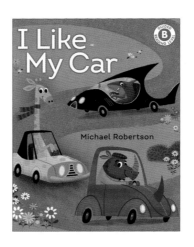

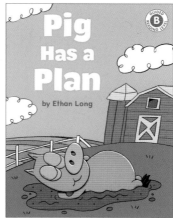

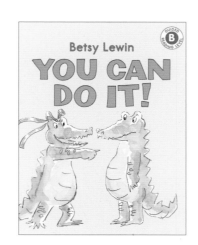